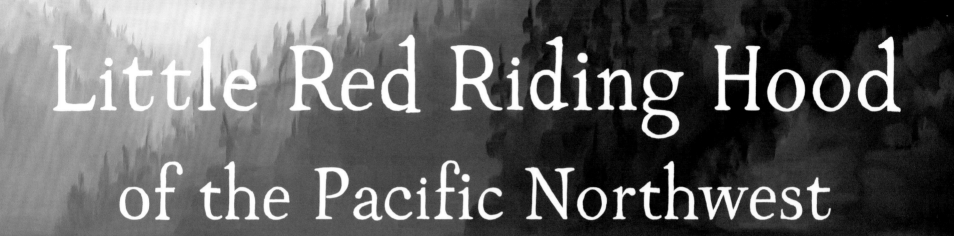

Little Red Riding Hood
of the Pacific Northwest

Marcia Crews   Illustrated by Jeremiah Trammell

little bigfoot
an imprint of sasquatch books
seattle, wa

Manufactured in China by C&C Offset Printing Co. Ltd.
Shenzhen, Guangdong Province, in July 2018

Published by Little Bigfoot, an imprint of Sasquatch Books

22 21 20 19 18   9 8 7 6 5 4 3 2 1

Editor: Christy Cox | Production editor: Bridget Sweet | Design: Anna Goldstein

Library of Congress Cataloging-in-Publication Data

Names: Crews, Marcia, author. | Trammell, Jeremiah, illustrator.
Title: Little Red Riding Hood of the Pacific Northwest / Marcia Crews ;
    illustrated by Jeremiah Trammell.
Description: Seattle : Little Bigfoot, [2018] | Summary: Little Red Riding
    Hood takes cherries to her great-grandmother's house for her birthday and
    encounters animals native to the Pacifc Northwest, including the much
    nicer great-grandson of the big bad wolf.
Identifiers: LCCN 2018000292 | ISBN 9781632171832 (hardcover)
Subjects: | CYAC: Animals--Northwest, Pacific--Fiction. | Northwest,
    Pacific--Fiction.
Classification: LCC PZ7.1.C743 Li 2018 | DDC [E]--dc23
LC record available at https://lccn.loc.gov/2018000292

ISBN: 978-1-63217-183-2

Sasquatch Books | 1904 Third Avenue, Suite 710 | Seattle, WA 98101
(206) 467-4300 | SasquatchBooks.com

Once upon a time, on the shore of the Salish Sea there stood a cabin made of driftwood, rocks, and seashells.

In this cabin lived a girl who was bold and brave,
and bursting with the spirit of adventure.

On the day of her great-grandmother's birthday, she picked a basket of fresh cherries to take to her party. This year her mother was letting her go all by herself.

"I was your age the first time I went to Great Grandma's house by myself," her mother said. "I wore this red velvet cape. And do you know what my mother called me?"

"What?" asked the girl.

"Little Red Riding Hood!" said her mother.

The girl wrapped the cape around her shoulders.

"It's beautiful," she said. "I'll wear it today, and you can call me Little Red Riding Hood too!"

"Now remember, Little Red Riding Hood," her mother said, "stick to the trail around the mountain. And watch out for wolves. I had trouble with a big bad one when I was your age."

"I will, Mama," Little Red said as she waved goodbye.

The trail to Great Granny's house wound through thick brush and towering old-growth trees that stretched to the sky. Little Red hadn't gone far when suddenly a large creature stepped out of the shadows.

"Hello, little girl," the creature said in a rough, tough voice. "Who are you, and where are you going on this fine day? Hmm?"

"I'm Little Red Riding Hood. I'm taking the trail around the mountain to give these cherries to my Great Granny for her birthday party. Who are you?"

"I'm Wolf," the creature replied.

"Not a big bad wolf!" Little Red exclaimed.

"Heavens, no. I'm a big *friendly* wolf," he said. "And you can get to Great Granny's faster if you take the shortcut over the mountain. Just follow that trail over there."

"Thank you, Wolf," Little Red said, and she set off along a trail that wound into the wild woods.

Once she was out of sight, the wolf growled to himself.

"So Great Granny's having a party, and I am not invited. We'll see about that!"

Off he dashed in the other direction as fast as he could go.

Little Red followed the shortcut trail through fragrant red cedar and hemlock trees until she came to a rushing river. Out of a lodge of woven sticks swam a plump brown beaver.

"Hello," Beaver said with a toothy grin. "Where are you going on this fine day?"

"I'm Little Red Riding Hood. I'm taking cherries to my Great Granny's house for her birthday party."

"A party for your Great Granny? I'd like to go too. May I come along with you? I can bring her this river stone that sparkles like gold in the sunlight," Beaver said with a happy slap of his tail.

Little Red nodded her head.

"The more the merrier," she said. "Great Granny would love a beautiful stone."

And off they went hopping from rock to rock across the river, following the trail deeper into the woods.

A cool breeze blew as the trail turned and twisted up the mountainside, through noble fir and pine trees, until they came to the mouth of a glistening blue ice cave.

Little Red peeked inside and found a roly-poly black bear cub snacking on huckleberries.

"Hello," Bear Cub said, licking juice off his nose. "Where are you two going on this fine day?"

"I'm Little Red Riding Hood. We're going to my Great Granny's house for her birthday party."

"A party? I'd like to go too. May I come along with you? I can bring her these sweet huckleberries."

Little Red nodded her head.

"The more the merrier," she said. "Great Granny loves huckleberries."

Off they went, following the trail up and up, past bare boulders and rocky peaks to a place where no trees grew. Here the air was crisp and cold, and the forest spread out below them. They came at last to a gap so wide they couldn't go another step.

"How will we get to the top?" asked Little Red.

"Grab hold of my horns and I'll pull you up!" called a shaggy white mountain goat.

Little Red grabbed onto his horns, and with a mighty pull-l-l-l, they all reached the top of the trail.

"Hello, travelers," Mountain Goat said. "What brings you three up here on this fine day?"

"I'm Little Red Riding Hood. We're going to my Great Granny's house for her birthday party."

"A party? I'd like to go too. May I come along with you? I can give her this blanket made from my cloud-white hair."

Little Red nodded her head.

"The more the merrier," she said. "A blanket would keep Great Granny warm all winter long."

Little Red looked at the steep slope on the other side of the mountain. "How will we get down?"

"It's easy," Mountain Goat said, shaking his shaggy head. "We'll slide down the snowfield. Follow me!"

"Whee!" cried Little Red and her friends as they slid down the sparkling snowfield. Bouncing around boulders, flying over stumps, spinning and rolling and laughing, they slipped and slid all the way to the bottom.

Brushing off the snow, the travelers found themselves
at the edge of a meadow dotted with wildflowers:
purple lupine, red paintbrush, pink shooting star, and
bluebell as bright as the sky above.

Little Red was searching for signs of the trail when a
frisky red fox came trotting up.

"Hello," Fox said, swishing her white-tipped tail. "Where are you four off to on this fine day?"

"I'm Little Red Riding Hood. My friends and I are going to my Great Granny's house for her birthday party."

"A party? I'd like to go too. May I come along with you? I can pick her a big bouquet of flowers!"

Little Red nodded her head.

"The more the merrier," she said. "Great Granny loves wildflowers. But I've lost the trail to her house."

"What does her house look like?" Fox asked.

"It's made of pine logs with a red roof and a fence as green as ferns," Little Red replied.

"I know where your Great Granny lives," said Fox. "It's just over that hill in a clearing in the woods."

Fox quickly picked a colorful bouquet of flowers and led the others over the hill.

"There's Great Granny's house!" cried Little Red.
Skipping up the steps, she knocked on the door.

Great Granny smiled with delight to see Little Red Riding Hood and her friends. In no time, decorations were hung and gifts were given. Everyone was having so much fun singing, dancing, and playing games that they didn't notice Wolf peering in the window, watching and waiting for just the right moment.

After the last game of Pin-the-Tail-On-the-Skunk, Little Red called everyone to the table.

"It's time for treats," she started to say, when suddenly . . .

BANG! CLANG! CRASH! SMASH!

the door flew open and in leaped the wolf!

"You're having a party I see," he growled, blocking the doorway. "But you forgot to invite me!"

"Oh, dear," said Little Red. "I'm so sorry."

"I'm here now and I'm hungry," snapped Wolf. "And I want to eat my favorite treat. Can you guess what it is?"

"US!" cried the animals in horror.

Wolf howled in glee. "And now I'm going to . . ."

"Munch us?" whimpered Beaver.

"Crunch us?" trembled Bear Cub.

"Gobble us up?" shivered Mountain Goat.

"Wolf us down in one gory gulp?" quivered Fox.

"No!" cried Wolf, creeping closer to the table. "What I'm going to do is . . .

give this beautiful blueberry birthday cake with raspberry icing and sparkly candles to Great Granny. *Surprise!*"

"This is the most incredible cake I've ever seen!" gasped Great Granny, cutting everyone a slice.

"I made it myself!" boasted Wolf. "Great-granddaddy Wolf was good at swallowing old ladies, but I'm the best at making sweet treats."

"Yummy!" munched Beaver.

"Delicious!"
crunched Bear Cub.

"Best ever!" gobbled Mountain Goat.

"More please," said Fox, wolfing down
a piece of cake in one glorious gulp.

"I'm sure you'd all be tasty, but everybody knows birthday cake is the most scrumptious treat in the whole wide world!" grinned Wolf, licking his plate.

"This is the best surprise ever!" said Little Red Riding Hood, giving Wolf a big happy hug. "We'll be sure to invite you to all our parties from now on."

That made Wolf so happy he took Little Red Riding Hood, Great Granny, and his new friends outside and taught them how to how-how-HOWL at the moon.

As the sky filled with stars, Little Red and Great Granny said goodnight to their friends and settled down together for a very special bedtime story.